THE VANISHING GRAN

When Lenny and Jake arrive to stay
with Lenny's gran in the country, she
is nowhere to be found. Has she been
kidnapped? Following clues provided
by a runaway girl who is camping out
in the empty house next door, Lenny
and Jake set off on the trail . . .

THE VANISHING GRAN

Hazel Townson

Illustrated by Philippe Dupasquier

Galaxy

CHIVERS PRESS
BATH

First published 1983
by
Andersen Press
This Large Print edition published by
Chivers Press
by arrangement with
Andersen Press Limited
1998

ISBN 0 7540 6029 2

British Library Cataloguing in Publication Data

Townson, Hazel,
    The Vanishing Gran. - Large print ed.
    1. Children's stories 2. Large type books
    I. Title
    823.9'14[J]

ISBN 0-7540-6029-2

Printed and bound in Great Britain by
Redwood Books, Trowbridge, Wiltshire

CONTENTS

For my first grandchild
JOHN DEREK HINDLE
born June 4th, 1982.

CHAPTER ONE

GRAN VANISHES

'You needn't think *I'm* having a baby-sitter!' cried Lenny Hargreaves indignantly. 'I'd rather swim the Channel in handcuffs and a ball-and-chain.'

Lenny's mother sighed.

'All right then, you'll have to go to your gran's for the weekend. I'm not leaving you in on your own, and that's that.'

Lenny's parents were planning a special wedding anniversary celebration which involved a dinner-dance at the hotel where they had spent their honeymoon. Lenny had already refused to go along to that, but was now even more disgusted at the thought of having Marcia Herbert, from next-door-but-two, bossing him around for the whole of a Saturday evening. Why, she was only a few years older than Lenny himself. The whole thing was unthinkable.

Actually, the weekend at Gran's was not a bad idea. Lenny got on fine with her, and often felt it was a pity she lived so far away. But he wasn't going to give in just like that. He frowned and pondered. Then he said, as if reluctantly, 'Okay then—provided Jake goes with me.'

Jake Allen was Lenny's best friend. The two of them spent as much time as possible together, usually at Lenny's house since Jake had five brothers and sisters. The weekend would be a treat for Jake as well, and together they would really be able to make the most of it.

So negotiations started. Lenny's gran agreed at once, but said it was a long way to come just for a weekend. Why

2

didn't the boys stay for a week, since it would be school holiday time? Or even a fortnight, come to that? The scheme grew into a major expedition.

Lenny's dad, who was a long-distance lorry-driver, dropped the boys off at Gran's one Wednesday morning, promising to pick them up on his way back from Carlisle in a fortnight's time.

Gran Hargreaves's semi-detached cottage stood at the end of a country lane. On one side stretched open moors, and on the other side the lane wound down for a mile into a little village. The feeling of space was tremendous.

'We can make as much noise as we like at my gran's,' Lenny had already promised Jake; and in fact, on the strength of this promise, Jake had brought along his mouth-organ and a sheepdog whistle that he'd bought at a jumble-sale, neither of which he was allowed to play with at home. Lenny, of course, had brought his conjuring set. He was hoping to impress his gran with the latest 'Jumping Bottle', not to mention the 'Multiplying Pennants' and 'Mysterious Message-slate'.

The boys piled out of the lorry and started off for the house, each clutching these most precious possessions, plus stacks of comics. Lenny's dad followed with the suitcases.

They found a notice on the front door of Gran's cottage, which said: GONE SHOPPING. BACK SOON.

'Sorry, lads, I can't wait,' said Lenny's dad, setting the suitcases down on the path. 'I'm late already. Have to be in Carlisle by half-past one.'

'That's okay, Dad. We'll mess about in the garden till she comes.'

'Yeah, well, not *too* much mess if you please! Righto then, see you in a fortnight. Be good, and give my love to your gran.'

Lenny's dad climbed back into his cab, reversed the lorry up the lane until he came to a turning place, then roared away with a last friendly wave.

After he had gone, the silence settled.

'Hey!' marvelled Jake. 'It *is* quiet, isn't it? Bet you can hear the grass growing. Even the house next door's empty.'

'So it is!' Only now did Lenny see the FOR SALE board, swinging in the wind from a gibbet-like post in next door's garden. 'Wonder what happened to old Mr Gribble? Deaf, he was, and ever so forgetful. I'll bet he's had to go and live with his married daughter.'

'Great! Now we can make even more noise!' To prove it, Jake charged off round the lawn, emitting blood-curdling whoops and yells.

Catching the fever, Lenny followed. Neither of them saw the startled face which peered cautiously out at them from a corner of one of next door's windows.

At last, they drew up panting and rosy-cheeked.

'Tell you what, I'm starving!' said Lenny. 'I could eat steak pudding, chips and peas, with apple pie and custard for afters and a bottle of coke to wash it down.'

'I could eat a pile of fat pork sausages and a great mound of creamy mashed potato, with beans in tomato sauce and chocolate cake to follow.'

'Let's have a wander round the back garden. We might find some raw carrots or strawberries or something.'

What they did find was a wheelbarrow, which immediately lured their thoughts from food. They began giving each other rides up and down the long path, then progressed to tipping each other out on to the grass. Finally, Lenny grazed his hands and decided he'd had enough.

'Hey, do you realise we've been here an hour and a half since my dad went?'

'I expect your gran's gossiping in the shops. My mum does that all the time.'

'Older folks ought to remember how hungry growing children get. Well at least I'm going in for a glass of water.'

'Isn't the door locked?'

'I know where the key is. See that little shelf in the back porch?' Lenny was already fishing out the back-door key and fitting it into the lock.

'Won't your gran mind us going in?'

''Course not. Anyway, it's her own fault. Back soon, she said, and now it's a quarter past two. I don't call that soon.'

The boys walked into the kitchen. On the table they found rows of freshly-baked buns on wire racks. The smell was delicious.

Lenny groaned. 'I wonder if she's counted them?'

He knew his gran would not mind if they took a bun each, but he felt that it would not stop at that. If the two of them once started on that batch of baking, they'd eat every crumb in sight. The only solution was total abstinence.

'Come on! We'd better go into the next room, out of temptation's way.'

But even here, the mouth-watering smell of baking lingered on. They had to do something to distract their minds from food. That was why Lenny fetched his conjuring set and asked Jake to help him practise his most ambitious project, 'The Vanishing Accomplice'.

'I've not really tried it out yet. I've only read up the instructions and that. You can be the accomplice and stand behind the curtain.'

Jake looked suspicious. 'What curtain?'

'We haven't got one yet, have we? Use your imagination. Here, stand by the window. As long as you're *behind*

me, that's the main thing.'

Lenny set up his lightweight, folding table, re-read his instructions and began:

'Ladies and gentlemen, may I introduce my accomplice, Jake Allen, who has kindly agreed to assist me with this experiment? As you will presently see, I shall make him vanish completely.'

Jake wasn't worried. He knew Lenny's usual standard of trick. Feeling slightly bored and enormously hungry, he stood by the window as requested.

Lenny picked up his magic baton and waved it through the air.

'Now we close the curtain—so!' He whisked an imaginary sheet of material in front of Jake's face. 'Then I say the magic words:

"Zin, Zan, Zamba, Zin, Zan, Zeer,
Let the one behind me disappear!" '

That was when Jake leapt smartly away from his spot behind the invisible curtain and jumped in front of Lenny.

'Boo! I've disappeared!'

Lenny was really cross. 'Idiot! You're supposed to stay behind me. How can I do the trick if you won't co-operate? Suppose there'd been someone else behind me? I could have made them disappear instead of you.'

'Well, as a matter of fact there was someone else behind you. I just heard your gran coming up the path.'

'Honest?' Lenny ran to the window, but there was nobody in sight. The only movement he noticed was the gate blowing slightly in the wind. So of course Jake was mistaken ... Or was he?

CHAPTER TWO

THE EMPTY HOUSE

Lenny's frown was both sulky and worried. He took his magic seriously and fully intended to make a career of it one day. He couldn't really have made his gran vanish, he supposed, but where was she? The whole journey to the shops and back should not take more than three quarters of an hour.

'It's time we went to look for her,' he decided. 'We'll fetch our luggage in, then walk down to the village stores. We can help her carry the shopping. She always has to walk, 'cause the bus

13

doesn't come this far.'

Jake groaned. 'It's a mile at least.'

'Do you good, a bit of fresh air and exercise.'

'On an EMPTY STOMACH?'

Lenny dragged in the last of the luggage, grabbed a couple of buns, then ushered Jake quickly outside.

As they began their walk, a furtive eye regarded them suspiciously from the bottom corner of one of next door's windows.

Apart from a rabbit which ran across the lane in front of them, the only moving things they met were birds. Not a human being in sight until they reached the village stores.

'Coxes Stores', however, was only too full of life. Lenny pushed his way into the crowd of shoppers and wriggled towards the counter.

'Excuse me—has Mrs Hargreaves been in today?'

Mrs Cox, the kindly owner of the shop, beamed over a box of apples.

'Yes, lovey, about half-past eleven. In a hurry, she was, on account of expecting her grandson. Here, that's you, isn't it? It's young Leonard, then! My, how you've grown!'

'Lenny,' insisted Lenny. (Goodness knew, that was bad enough, but Leonard—!)

'Well, your granny will be home long since. She said she was going straight back to make your dinner. It'll be getting cold by now.' Mrs Cox began to giggle. 'Oh, she hasn't half got a surprise for you!'

'But she's not there . . .' began Lenny, his voice drowned immediately by an impatient customer.

'Tell you what, I'll have four nice oranges, Mrs Cox. Oh, and how much is the boiled ham this week? Give me a couple of slices of that, then, love, and a pound of thin pork sausages.'

Lenny sighed. No use expecting help from this direction. He struggled out of the shop again, Mrs Cox calling distractedly after him, 'Be seeing you then, lovey. You'll be coming in for your toffees and that I expect.'

Lenny pulled a face at Jake, who was waiting outside.

'She disappeared between here and home over two hours ago.'

'Crikey!' Jake was impressed. 'She must be more of a magician than you. There's nothing between here and there except an empty lane. Maybe that trick of yours . . .'

'You're forgetting something,' Lenny

cut in sharply. 'There's that empty house next door. She must have gone in there.'

'What for?'

'I dunno. Feed the cat, or water the plants or something.'

'Empty, you said. No cat, no plants, nothing.'

'Funny thing is, I got the feeling there was somebody in there when we went past.'

'Here, just suppose—just suppose she *is* in there . . . as a prisoner?'

Lenny stopped. 'Kidnapped, or something?'

'Why not? Stranger things have happened, especially in my maths homework. Anyway, just think of Erica Carr.'

Lenny could not deny the strength of this argument. Erica Carr, who sat next to Lenny in class, had been captured by villains not so long ago, and rescued by Jake and Lenny. If it could happen once, it could happen again.

'Right, what are we waiting for?' Lenny started off at once towards the empty house.

'I'll just check my gran's again in case she's come home since we left.'

'Grab another couple of buns whilst you're at it.'

At last, fortified by further food, the two boys marched up the path next door and peered in at the front downstairs window. There was nothing to be seen except a thick layer of dust beyond the finger-marked pane.

'Looks a bit one-star.'

'Come on, let's try round the back.'

The garden was the same size and shape as Lenny's gran's garden, but there the resemblance ceased. This one was overgrown with knee-high grass and thistles, shapeless privet and clumps of fireweed. There were bits of blown-down roof-tile scattered on the path and a broken bottle on the back doorstep.

'My gran's not been here,' declared Lenny. 'She'd have picked up that broken glass, for a start.'

'Not if she was bound and gagged at the time. Hey, look! The kitchen window's broken.'

It was true. A whole pane of glass was

18

missing. The gap had evidently been boarded up with a sheet of plywood, but this sheet now lay inside on the kitchen floor. Lenny leaned into the gap and peered around the kitchen. As he did so, a strange thing happened. A rosy apple, with a clean, white bite out of it, began to roll slowly across the floor.

Jake had seen it, too. The boys looked from the apple to each other. Then Jake nodded and Lenny started to climb quietly in through the gap.

It was not an easy climb. You had to step into the sink first, catching your shins on the taps. Then you had to sit on the edge of the sink, lowering your legs and launching yourself towards the floor. The water must not have been turned off either, for Lenny's seat felt decidedly damp by the time he'd arrived.

Lenny picked up the apple, his mouth beginning to water.

'Somebody's only just bitten into that.'

Even as he spoke there was a scuffling noise behind an inner door, followed by the sound of soft footsteps retreating rapidly upstairs.

'Kids!' sneered Jake, his courage renewed. He and Lenny bounded up the bare wooden staircase.

At the top, a bedroom door slammed in their faces. Someone was leaning on the other side, but the two boys soon managed to force the door open. When they burst into the bedroom they found, to their surprise, a solitary girl no bigger than themselves. She wore trousers and a thick jumper, though the day was warm, and her hair was gathered back in an elastic band. Her face was dirty and quite fierce-looking as she glared at the boys and said: 'I've not done anything wrong.'

'You're trespassing,' said Lenny.

'How do *you* know?'

''Cause my gran lives next door. This house belongs to Mr Gribble.'

'No, it doesn't, then. He died.'

'Well, it doesn't belong to you.'

'I've as much right to come here as you have.'

'We're looking for his gran,' Jake butted in. 'She's vanished.'

'Well, she's not the only one. What

do you think *I'm* doing here?'

'You've run away from home? How daft can you get?'

The girl's cheeks turned pink. 'Why don't you two clear off and mind your own business?'

'You can't live here with no bed and nothing to eat and no fire or anything. You must be barmy,' decided Lenny.

'Anyway, somebody's sure to find you sooner or later,' added Jake. 'The house agent'll come. He'll be bringing people to look the place over, and even if *they* don't see you, somebody will buy it in the end and move in.'

'She could be the resident ghost,' grinned Lenny.

The pink cheeks turned to fiery red. 'I suppose you think only boys can do anything worth doing? Well, let me tell you I'm not half as soft as you think.' The girl leapt over to a large fitted cupboard and threw open its door. Inside the cupboard was a sleeping-bag, plastic crockery and cutlery, a saucepan, a biscuit tin, a loaf of bread, soap and a towel.

'Hey, not bad!' Lenny was impressed.

'You could last a few days, at any rate. What did you run away for?'

'I'll bet it was your mum,' guessed Jake as the girl refused to reply. 'Do this, don't do that, don't answer back. If it was, you should take no notice. Everybody's mum's like that. You should hear mine on a Friday night when she's got five lots of hair to wash and the youngest two to bath and all the ironing for the weekend ...'

'What's your name?' cut in Lenny, who was only too familiar with the Allens' domestic scene.

'What's yours?'

'He's Jake and I'm Lenny.'

There was quite a pause before the girl said, 'I'm Jackie.'

'That's a boy's name.'

'No, it's not. It's short for Jacqueline.'

Lenny felt a sudden twinge of sympathy. Leonard and Jacqueline! Honestly, the grown-ups didn't deserve to win.

'How long have you been here?'

'As long as your nose!'

'Oh, don't be so touchy; we might be able to help you. Living next door, and that. We could save you bits of our meals.'

(If we ever get any, thought Jake).

Jackie relented. 'I only came this morning. But I'm going to stay for weeks. I'm going to give them a real good scare.'

'Yeah, if you say so. But it could be boring, sitting up here by yourself all the time. Why don't you team up with us? You could help us find my gran.'

'She really has vanished.' Jake began the tale of the magic trick and all that had happened since.

'You mean your gran's that Mrs Hargreaves who lives next door? I've seen her this morning. A funny-looking man came and took her off in a car, if you call that vanishing.'

'You WHAT?'

'I told you she'd been kidnapped,' Jake said sadly. Now there would be no supper, either.

CHAPTER THREE

THE CRIME IS REPORTED

'I don't suppose you noticed the make or the registration number of that car?' Lenny asked without hope.

Jackie's chin came up. 'As a matter of fact, I did. It was a dark blue Avenger, and I remember the letters because they spelt HAM. HAM 125T.'

Jake's face lit up with admiration. 'Hey, Jackie, that's great! We'll easily trace it now.'

Lenny, however, was looking suspicious. 'That came out a bit pat.

You're not having us on, are you? Because if you are . . .' Lenny left a threatening pause before he went on: 'We happen to know my gran went to Cox's Stores about half-past eleven. So how could she have been picked up in a car?'

'It could have been after she got home from the shop,' Jake pointed out.

'Then why didn't she take the notice down from the door?'

'Perhaps she didn't have time. He just caught her and whisked her off. Maybe he was just going to burgle the house when she walked in.'

Lenny grunted scornfully, but he was thinking hard. There was something in what Jake said. 'What time was it when you saw them?'

'My watch has stopped,' admitted Jackie grudgingly. Well, not even boys could make everything go right all the time.

Lenny gave Jackie a calculating look. Then he decided. 'Come on, then. We can't sit here. We've got to catch up with that car. Come with us and identify it properly.'

27

'I've already identified it. What more do you want, the colour of the ashtray?'

'Fair enough. Sit here by yourself in the dust, then, not even knowing what time it is. See you one of these days. Maybe.'

Lenny turned towards the stairs. Jake hesitated, as though he were going to speak to Jackie, then thought better of it and followed his friend. But at the last minute Jackie said: 'He was wearing blue overalls, and he had a great bush of black hair.'

'Sounds like a wig,' said Jake as he and Lenny struggled out by the kitchen window and started off down the lane.

Jackie did not follow, but watched them wistfully from the window. Then she picked up the bitten apple which Lenny had set down on the windowsill, polished it on her jeans and took another bite.

'We can't just hike around the countryside looking for a car,' grumbled Jake. 'It could be at John-o'-Groats by now.'

'We're going to the police station. It's

that little house across from the church. There's only one constable for a village this size, and that's where he lives.'

Jake groaned, remembering another occasion when he and Lenny had tangled with the police. 'He won't believe us.'

'Yes, he will. They take things more seriously in the country. Anyway, he'll know my gran. Everybody knows everybody else round here.'

'You think that girl's telling the truth, then?'

'Yeah, I think she is, 'cause she knows if she's not we'll jolly well tell on *her*. Anyway, my gran's got to be *somewhere*. She wouldn't have left us with no dinner unless something was up. She's a great one for regular meals.'

The police station looked just like any other house, except for the POLICE notice over the door and the poster in the window showing a thief running off with an old lady's handbag. Lenny marched boldly up the path and rang the bell.

A woman in an apron came to the door, drying her hands on a towel. She

was accompanied by a toddler eating a jam tart, or at any rate pressing it to his face.

'Is the policeman in, please?'

'No, he's not,' said the woman, trying to guide the jam tart to the right bit of face.

'We wanted to see him urgently,' Lenny went on. 'It's about a missing person.'

'Could be a kidnapping, or something even worse,' Jake added with relish. Maybe he overdid the drama, for the woman's hand slipped and the jam tart skidded into the toddler's eye. The toddler howled with anguish.

'Oh, we know all about the kidnapping. (Hush now, Raymond, I can't hear myself think!) In fact the constable's gone off to Powerby now to help with the investigations. (Raymond, stop it! Now you've got jam all down my tights.) She's been spotted in Powerby, poor soul. Somebody saw her in a car with a man.'

'Yes, we know the number of the car.'

'You do?'

'And we've got a description of the driver.'

'Well, you'd best get in touch with the police right away. Best thing would be if you went into Powerby. They'll want to talk to you. (Oh, Raymond, go and get another one, then.). The Powerby bus will be along in a minute. Get off at the Odeon and the police station's only just round the corner. It'll only take you ten minutes. You got some money for your fares?'

'Yes, thanks.' Lenny jingled his holiday spending money in his pocket.

'Well, you tell all you know. Don't leave anything out. Because there isn't half a fuss going on over that poor dear, and I'm sure . . .'

What the policeman's wife was sure of they would never know, for at that moment Raymond reappeared with a second jam tart upside down on his hair and the bus came into sight.

The bus had scarcely left the village behind when a strange thing happened. Jake, who was sitting next to the window, spotted a big, detached house standing well back from the road. Just inside the driveway of this house a car was parked. It was a dark blue Avenger, registration HAM 125T.

CHAPTER FOUR

FACE TO FACE WITH THE CRIMINAL

Never had two passengers disembarked so quickly from a country bus
'That's not the Odeon!' the driver shouted, but our heroes were already gone. They had dodged between the gate-posts of this handsome house and were now cautiously homing in on the kidnapper's empty vehicle.

'This is a great place for a hideout,' whispered Lenny. 'Nothing for miles. We were lucky to spot the car.'

'I spotted it, and it wasn't luck, it was good management. Is she rich, your gran?'

'Nah! My dad's always wondering if she can manage on her pension. She does all right, though. She makes a bit of money painting pictures. Country scenes and that.'

'Wonder why she got kidnapped, then?'

'Perhaps she knows something. Perhaps she was sitting in the country one day, quietly painting a picture, when she saw a crime being committed. Or maybe she's been mistaken for somebody else. My dad says she looks like Mrs Thatcher in her best blue suit.'

'You never said she was an artist.'

'Well, she only took it up after my grandad died. Something to fill the time in, I expect. She says it's only a hobby.'

'What if she turns out to be famous, like Grandma Moses?'

'She won't turn out to be anything if we don't rescue her, that's for sure.'

'We can't just walk up the drive and knock at the door. He'll be watching. I'll bet he's got binoculars. I'll bet he's watching us right now.'

'See that PUBLIC FOOTPATH sign? The path runs right along the side

of the house. That's the way we'll go.'

'So that he'll think we're just a couple of kids out for a hike.'

'We'll saunter past the place and spy it out.'

Trying their best to look like happy wanderers without a care in the world, Jake and Lenny started off along the footpath.

'Point your arm in the opposite direction, as if we're interested in something miles away.' Distracting the audience's attention was something Lenny had learnt to do very early in his magical career. ('Let everyone concentrate on the empty cylinder you hold aloft in one hand, while you gently shake the coin down the sleeve of your other arm.')

As they drew level with the side gate of the house, both boys' hearts beat faster. What would they do if the kidnapper suddenly opened the door and came after them? Maybe they should have stayed on the Powerby bus after all, and left the tricky bits to the police.

'There he is!' Lenny grabbed Jake and pulled him down in the nick of time, as a black-haired man in overalls suddenly appeared in the back garden. Where had he sprung from? Surely he couldn't have been hiding behind the dustbin?

Now the man ran to the wall of the house, flattened himself against it and began to edge cautiously along towards the french windows.

'That's him all right! Did you ever see anybody act more like a criminal in your life?'

'If he's hurt my gran, I'll . . . !'

'Ssssh!'

39

Breathlessly, the boys watched as the dark-haired man in overalls gently undid the catch of the french windows, cast a hunted look around him and slipped indoors, leaving the windows slightly ajar.

Now the question was, should they go in after him? Lenny felt that if they went off to fetch help, his poor old gran could be minced up for cat-food by the time they got back. So maybe they should risk it.

Meanwhile, back in the late Mr Gribble's empty house, Jackie sat on her sleeping-bag and chewed miserably at a hunk of dry bread. It wasn't much fun. Maybe if she hadn't met those two boys the whole thing would have seemed more of an adventure, but after they had gone things turned very dull and boring. The trouble was, Jackie badly needed companionship, something absorbing to fill in the empty holidays. That was one reason why she had run away in the first place. All her pleas to be allowed to play with the farm family up the lane had been

40

ignored, and there was nobody else for miles. After only two months she could tell she wasn't going to like living in the country. London had been much more exciting.

Jackie sighed and wandered back to the window. Where had Jake and Lenny got to now? Had they sorted out the business of the car? They were in the middle of a real adventure, and if only she hadn't been so proud she could have joined in. She could have made friends with those two. Jackie hacked off another hunk of bread, took a bite, then threw down the rest in disgust. Bread was horrible without butter and jam. Finally she came to a decision. Rolling her possessions up inside the sleeping-bag, she tied the bundle with string and started downstairs. She was going back home.

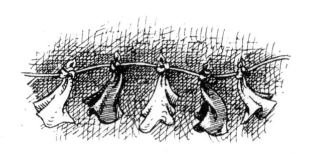

CHAPTER FIVE

THE FLYING PENNANTS

'If we go in after him,' reasoned Lenny in a whisper, 'he could easily trap us'

'Lock us up, you mean?'

'Lock us in with my gran. She'll be upstairs or in the cellar.'

'Well, suppose you go in, and I go for the police.'

One withering glance from Lenny put paid to that idea.

'You know the rules—always stick together in an emergency, and use your brains, not your brawn.'

'Go on, then,' urged Jake sarcastically.

'We'll try a bit of magic,' replied Lenny importantly. 'He's gone in and left the french windows ajar, so he's going to come out again. We'll catch him as he comes out. Take him by surprise.'

'Your magic stuff's all at your gran's . . .' began Jake, but he was wrong. Lenny was already drawing from his sleeve a bit of flesh-coloured tape which he handed to his friend. 'Here, take hold of this. Don't move from your side of the window, and don't let go whatever happens.'

Lenny ducked and ran to the other side of the french window. As he went, so the tape unwound from the depths of Lenny's sleeve, dragging forth little silk flags by the dozen, all in different colours. It was one of Lenny's favourite magic tricks, put on with his jersey this morning, which he had hoped to spring upon his startled gran at lunch. Jake lowered his end of the tape to the ground, as he saw Lenny had done, and crouched there waiting.

It seemed a long, uncomfortable wait. They could hear the kidnapper in the room beyond them, rattling cutlery as if preparing a meal. Jake almost

groaned aloud with hunger, envying even Lenny's kidnapped gran if she was about to be fed.

Then all of a sudden, so that he almost caught the boys napping, the kidnapper made a hasty exit carrying a bulging haversack.

Lenny's end of the tape came swiftly up to knee height, Jake's end followed, the kidnapper rushed right into it and fell flat on his face on the path, festooned with coloured pennants like a royal visit.

'Sit on him!' cried Lenny, deftly demonstrating what he meant.

Their victim struggled, gasped and spluttered as Jake sank down on to his shoulders.

'What have you done with my gran?' yelled Lenny, bouncing up and down on the poor man's middle. Even if he had been able to speak, the man would have had nothing to tell, for he had never even heard of Lenny's gran, much less kidnapped her.

Goodness knows what might have happened next if the two boys had been left alone with their victim. The man was not only strong but desperate, and had jerked the tape—(fastened to the inside of Lenny's jersey by a safety-pin)—so hard that the jersey had torn and was now unravelling at an alarming rate. Lenny could feel the draught growing stronger across his back.

But the situation was saved. At that moment a car drew up with a screech on the road outside the house. Doors slammed and running footsteps grew louder.

'Here come the police!' thought Lenny. 'And about time, too!'

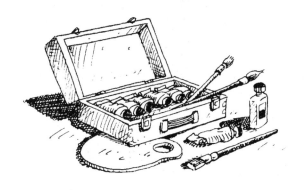

CHAPTER SIX

EMERGENCY HELP

Maud Hargreaves had taken up
painting when her husband died, partly
to fill in the time, but partly also
because it was something she had
always wanted to do. She bought herself
an easel, a palette, canvasses, oil-paints
and brushes, and began working away
in the evenings with only herself to
please. Then the vicar happened to
drop by whilst she was finishing 'A View
Across the Moors'. He was so pleased
with what he saw that he asked Maud to
paint a similar scene for him, to hang in

his study, where he could see it—and find inspiration—when writing his sermons.

Other people saw it, too. The vicar's visitors admired the painting, asked where it had come from, and eventually sought out Maud to order something for themselves. Then their visitors admired in turn, and Maud Hargreaves began to build up quite a reputation. She did not boast to her family about her accomplishment, partly because she could not believe that her success would last. She simply said she was happy with her 'little hobby'. And then, one day, she realised that she had sold so many pictures that she was getting quite rich. She decided to take driving lessons. If her son could drive a lorry all over Europe, surely she could manage a few quiet lanes for little country jaunts in summer? That way she would be able to find other, even more beautiful scenes to paint. Finally, after four attempts, she managed to pass her driving test. Then she bought a car—a second-hand, yellow Ford. Still she said nothing to her family, but arranged to have the car delivered on the day of her grandson's visit. What a surprise it would be for Jake and Lenny, and what fun for her to be able to take the boys out for rides!

Jed Soames from the garage—a lively lad with a great bush of black hair— spruced up the car for her and delivered it to her gate at half-past ten on the Wednesday morning of Lenny's visit. Maud climbed into the car and set off with Jed to drive him back to the garage. Next she called at the village stores and caused quite a sensation. Even the busy Mrs Cox came out to admire the vehicle, which Maud loaded up with shopping before starting out for some eggs at the nearest farm. So far, so good. Everything was working out to plan, and Maud felt excited at the prospect of astounding her young visitors.

Then things began to go wrong.

As she drove, Maud noticed the figure of a woman running distractedly along the roadside. Why, it was that nice Mrs Fox who had recently moved into the big house at the cross roads. Maud pulled up and wound down the window.

'Anything wrong?'

Mrs Fox turned a fearful, tear-stained face to Maud and began to pour out her tale of woe. Her daughter, Annabel, had disappeared.

'One minute she was in the garden, the next minute she'd gone. Somebody said they'd seen her drive into the village in a car with a man. The times I've told her never to take lifts from strangers! So I got into my car to chase after her, and my car wouldn't start. I tried to ring my husband, but he's not in his office. So I've just rushed out without thinking really, trying to find

out what's happened.'

'Here, you'd better get in,' Maud said kindly. She had met Mrs Fox a few times at church functions, and had thought her a sensible woman. She wouldn't panic like this unless there were a very good cause.

'We'll drive around for a bit and see if we can find her. If not, we'll call at the police station to report Annabel missing. Then I'll drive you into Powerby to your husband's office. He'll probably be back there by then.'

'Oh, Mrs Hargreaves, you're such a comfort! I don't know what I'd have done without you!'

Of course, Maud had not forgotten that her visitors were expected, but this was an emergency. There was a note on her door, and her visitors would just have to wait.

Maud and Mrs Fox drove around for quite a while, enquiring of everyone they met. Lots of people said they had seen Annabel, riding on a haycart, mending a bicycle, climbing a tree in the woods, buying ice-cream from a van, or playing hopscotch in the school yard with a couple of boys. All these stories had to be checked, taking time and getting nowhere in the end, which just goes to show that ordinary people have far more imagination than they are given credit for.

At last the two women realised they would need help. They told their tale to the village constable, who then went into Powerby with them to repeat the story and obtain instructions from his superiors. This took even more time, and it was well into afternoon before the woman finally arrived at Mr Fox's office.

Mr Fox had just come in. He decided to abandon work for the day and take his wife home. So at last Maud was able to return to her visitors.

CHAPTER SEVEN

SCREAMS AND TEASPOONS

Lenny was mistaken. The footsteps he had heard were not those of the police, but of Mr and Mrs Fox, who had just driven home from Mr Fox's office in Powerby. This house was theirs, and they had come home in obedience to police instructions, to wait for news of their missing daughter Annabel.

The first thing the Foxes heard was the commotion going on in the back garden. Was Annabel already home? Excitedly, they ran round the side of the house—only to find a strange man lying face downwards on their path, swathed in coloured flags and topped by two

54

dishevelled boys. It was a bewildering sight. Imagine going home yourself to such an unexpected welcome. Mr and Mrs Fox did not know what to think. But of course the disappearance of their daughter was uppermost in their minds, so when they heard Lenny yell something about a kidnapper, they immediately concluded that this man had made off with Annabel. Angrily, Mr Fox took charge. Sending his wife into the house to telephone for help, he seized the prostrate man and tried to shake answers out of him.

'What have you done with my daughter? Where is she? If you've so much as broken her fingernail . . .'

Lenny's victim managed to wriggle his head free and gasp: 'Here, steady on! If you leave off shaking me, I'll try and explain. I don't know what I'm supposed to have done with all your blooming relatives—first his gran and then your daughter; goodness knows who it'll be next—but I haven't seen a soul all day till these two come along and tripped me up.'

Of course, Mr Fox didn't believe a

word of this. Nor did Lenny and Jake.

'He was spotted!' yelled Lenny indignantly. 'Someone in the house next door saw him dragging my gran into his car.'

'They even got the number.'

'What car? I haven't *got* a car!'

'Take no notice of him!' Jake advised Mr Fox. 'His car's right there in your drive. You must have seen it.'

'Just a minute—!' pleaded the bewildered Mr Fox. But before he could say more there came a piercing scream from within the house.

'Annabel!' cried Mr Fox.

'Gran!' cried Lenny.

'Burglars!' cried Mrs Fox, rushing out of the house again in frightened indignation. 'We've been robbed, George! All the silver, even the teaspoons.'

'Teaspoons?' Lenny remembered hearing the clink of cutlery earlier on. Now he reached out and pulled the haversack of the kidnapper towards him. It was stuffed with silver.

'I can explain everything,' the man began hastily. 'I'm just setting up a silver-cleaning service in this area, and

you know how difficult it is to get a new business going these days. I thought if I gave everybody's silver a nice, surprise clean for free, then maybe they would . . .'

'This is a nightmare! It isn't really happening!' muttered Mrs Fox faintly.

'What's all this got to do with Annabel, that's what I want to know,' cried Mr Fox, dragging the burglar into the house. Jake and Lenny followed, and although Mr Fox hadn't a clue who these boys were he felt it might be wisest to keep all the pieces of this puzzle in one place. Clearer minds than his would have to come and sort it out.

'There's no sign of Annabel here,' announced a distraught Mrs Fox. 'I've searched the house.'

'Don't worry, dear; we'll drag it all out of them in time. The police will be here soon. Perhaps you'd better go and put the kettle on.'

Lenny felt suddenly uncomfortable. Mr Fox had said 'them'. It sounded as though he thought Lenny and Jake were villains, too. Jake, on the other hand, could only feel enormously

cheered at the thought of the kettle going on. Maybe there would be biscuits to go with the tea—and possibly even a sandwich or a great, thick slice of fruit cake.

'Kidnapping,' said Mr Fox, 'is the worst crime in the book. In my opinion, no punishment is strong enough . . .'

'Hear, hear!' interrupted Lenny. 'Especially when it's a poor old-age pensioner who can't defend herself.'

Mrs Fox turned at the kitchen door. 'A *what*? I honestly think I shall go mad quite soon. I have never lived through such a day in the whole of my life. George, will you tell me slowly, in words of one syllable if possible, exactly what has happened?'

George Fox took a deep breath.

'Well, dear, it seems this—this person stole your car to begin with . . . '

'Then he must be a mechanical genius. I couldn't get the thing further than the end of our drive this morning. It just stopped and wouldn't start again.'

Jake turned wide eyes upon Mrs Fox. 'You mean—that's *your* car out there? That dark blue Avenger, registration number HAM 125T?'

Now it was Lenny's turn to feel confused. Was this lady his gran's kidnapper after all? If she'd disguised herself as a man, in overalls and dark wig, it was just possible. In that case, he and Jake had walked right into a trap. All this play-acting about burglars was just to put them off their guard.

'Well, it's time we were off now,' said Lenny, dragging Jake towards the french windows. But Mr Fox was there before him.

'Oh, no you don't! You're not going anywhere, my boy, until we've got all this sorted out.'

CHAPTER EIGHT

THE WANDERER'S RETURN

Tired and weary after her long trek from the village, Jackie reached home at last. Her feelings about this were mixed. There would be a lot of explaining to do, and she would probably get into trouble for running away in the first place. But maybe, after a little scare, her parents would see her point about needing friends. It wasn't so bad during term time, as she'd made a few new friends in school, but they all lived miles away and could only visit on rare occasions. There were boys at the nearby farm, but her mother had forbidden her to play with them.

Jackie sighed. Probably all she had

done was to make her parents even more determined to keep an eye on her. Now they'd probably lock her in the house all summer. Miserably, she hitched up her bundle and turned in at the front gate.

Lenny saw her first as she came round the corner towards the french windows.

'Hey, there's Jackie!' As soon as he said it, the penny dropped.

'Jackie?' echoed Jake. Then he turned to Mr Fox.

'I'll bet your daughter Annabel tells whopping lies.'

Much later, when all the emotional fuss was over, Lenny complained: 'I wish you'd make your mind up what you're called.'

'I'm called Annabel,' the girl admitted, pulling a face. 'Only I think Jackie sounds a lot less soppy.'

'All right, I can understand that,' agreed Lenny, who had once thought of calling himself Alfonso after seeing a particularly exciting bandit film.

'But what about this car, then?'

Annabel's chin came up. 'It was your

own fault. You shouldn't have talked down to me, just because I was a girl. You were so sure I wouldn't have noticed that car registration. I thought, "Right, I'll show 'em!" So I told you the first registration that came into my head. It happened to be my mum's.'

'Well, you'd no business to,' cried Jake. 'You've made us waste all this time now, and we could have been saving his gran's life.'

'Yes, she might have been put on a plane for Timbuctoo by now. If we'd gone straight to the police station as we were told, instead of following your false clue . . .'

'Police?' echoed Mr Fox. 'Heavens, I'd forgotten all about them! I'd better ring them up and tell them Annabel's safe after all.'

'Don't forget about the burglar, George.'

Silence descended on the room as Mr Fox dialled the number. Then everyone listened in unashamedly to the nearest half of the conversation, which proved intriguing. Something else was obviously wrong. When Mr Fox finally put down the telephone, five faces turned questioningly towards him.

George Fox turned to the burglar.

'When you've finished your tea,' he said politely, 'I'll drive you to the station. Apparently the police have their hands full just now, so they can't come and get you. Two more kidnappings. Some woman just rang in to say her grandson and his friend had disappeared.'

Lenny turned pale, then pink.

'Hear that, Jake? My gran's okay!'

'We'd better get back for our dinner, then,' said Jake.

'I'd dearly love to know just what you have been up to,' declared Mr Fox, looking more suspicious than a donkey with a plastic carrot.

'Catching your burglar, that's what!' cried Annabel warmly. 'Not to mention persuading me to come back home. If it hadn't been for them, I might still have been missing.'

'We asked her to team up with us,' explained Jake.

'The offer still stands,' said Lenny generously. 'Could Jackie—I mean, Annabel—come back with us, please? My gran won't mind. We're here for a fortnight. She could come every day if she wants. She could come to our special conjuring session.'

'She could even be the Vanishing Accomplice,' Jake said happily.